W9-BBZ-335

Ale Barba

WHEN YOUR ELEPHANT COMES to PLAY

PHILOMEL BOOKS

For you, because you never seem to give up on me.

PHILOMEL BOOKS

An imprint of Penguin Random House LLC
375 Hudson Street, New York, NY 10014

Philomel Books is a registered trademark of Penguin Random House LLC.

Library of Congress Cataloging-in-Publication Data
Barba, Ale, author, illustrator. When your elephant comes to play / Ale Barba. pages cm Summary: "A young boy must figure out how to entertain his large elephant friend"—Provided by publisher. [1. Elephants—Fiction. 2. Humorous stories.]
I. Title. PZ7.1.B37Wh 2016 [Fic]—dc23 2015002932
Manufactured in China by RR Donnelley Asia Printing Solutions Ltd.
ISBN 978-0-399-16312-8
1 3 5 7 9 10 8 6 4 2

Edited by Jill Santopolo | Design by Semadar Megged | Text set in 21-point Metallophile Sp8
The art was done using cotton paper, acrylics, paint rollers and brushes.

Author's note: It's important to say that, in addition to the physical materials listed above, these illustrations are also made up of the love and hard work of the talented team at this publishing house. This artwork wouldn't shine if it weren't for them.

On Wednesdays, an elephant comes to my house.

Her name is Prudence. You might think it's easy being friends with an elephant. It's not.

First of all, you should never offer an elephant a
slice of your dad's famous double chocolate cake,

just out of the oven.

At least not if you want to eat some yourself.
Or ever use your kitchen again.

You might be tempted to ask your elephant

to help with your chores.

That would not be a smart thing to do.

And if your elephant is hot, you should absolutely
not invite her to swim in your pool.

At least not if you're planning on swimming yourself.

And whatever you do, do not ask
your elephant to come play in your
tree house.

Unless you want it to be
a ground house instead.

Don't ever,

under any circumstances,

invite your elephant to jump on the bed.

She'll definitely wake up your baby sister. Along with everyone else in your neighborhood.

But the one thing you should *always* do with your elephant is give her a hug.

There's nothing quite like a hug from an elephant.

And then you can get ready for Thursdays,

when your alligator comes to play . . .